HARRY POTTER

BATHROOM READER

The Unofficial Book of Harry Potter Facts and Trivia

Jay Stone

Published in the United States of America.

[E2]

Table of Contents

Heavens to Betsy

Less than 10 books in the history of time have sold more than 100 million copies. *Harry Potter and the Philosopher's Stone* is one of those books.

Also on the list is *Don Quixote, A Tale of Two Cities, The Lord of the Rings, The Hobbit,* and *Alice in Wonderland.*

Author J.K. Rowling is the first author to have earned more than one billion dollars from her writing. She's also the first author to give away so much money to charity, that she lost her billionaire status.

She even founded her own charity called Lumos. It focuses on helping disadvantaged children worldwide.

The Hug of Death

This happened in the Deathly Hallows movie, part 2. About 1 hour and 40 minutes into the film Voldemort leans over and hugs Malloy. This was not called for in the script. It was improvised by actor Ralph Fiennes.

Tom Felton, not knowing what to do next because this wasn't part of the script, stopped moving and looked surprised. This shot made it into the final cut of the film because director David Yates thought it looked genuine and amazing.

The Weasley-Moody Connection

Alastor Moody, the famous Auror, and investigator of Dark Arts crimes, was played in the movies by actor Brendan Gleeson.

Bill Weasley, the eldest of the Weasley boys, was played by Brendan Gleeson's son, Domhnall Gleeson.

This was Domhnall's first big break into movies. He would later act in more great movies. *True Grit, Dredd,* and even *Star Wars: Episode VII: The Force Awakens.*

The Hardest Scene to Film

The scene in Deathly Hallows part 2 with the "Seven Harrys" was so hard to film that it took more than 90 takes to get right.

Because of the complex cameras and expensive lighting, it can take filmmakers up to 30 minutes just to set up a single shot.

This means the "Seven Harrys" event could have taken more than 45 hours to film correctly. That's more than five days of work just to film one scene.

Voldemort the Narcissist

Did you know the actor who portrayed Young Tom Riddle (Hero Fiennes-Tiffin, yes *Hero* is real name) is the nephew of the actor who played Voldemort?

Ralph Fiennes did not specifically ask the director to hire his nephew. Hero auditioned just like everybody else, but his uncanny resemblance to his uncle was "a clincher," according to director David Yates.

Yates also said there was a "wonderful haunted quality," about Hero. You might say he was destined to land the part.

Much ado About Hair Color

In the Harry Potter books, the hair color of the character Tonks is described bubble gum pink. For the movies the color pink was used as a theme for Delores Umbridge.

The filmmakers did not want the audience to be confused. If they saw Tonks' pink hair they might think the two characters were working together or maybe friends.

In the end they decided to change Tonks' hair to purple.

Side Business

Actress Evanna Lynch isn't just famous for her role as Luna Lovegood. She's also an accomplished fashion model and accessories designer.

The radish earrings that Luna wears in the films were designed and created by the actress herself.

Evanna beat out more than 15,000 other girls to land the role of Luna. She heard about the open casting call on a Harry Potter fan site. While she was already something of a pen pal with writer J.K. Rowling, Rowling was unaware that Evanna had landed the role until the producers handed her the final casting list. She was reportedly quite pleased with the selection.

That's one Expensive Family Tree

J.K. Rowling's time, which is valued at over £5 million/week, spent hours designing the Black family tree which is seen in the Order of the Phoenix movie.

She created more than 70 unique individuals, along with family connections, and character background stories.

Detailed information about the history and relations between each family remember were created. Fans occasionally ask Rowling to release it as a non-fiction book.

Don't ask This Character to the Dance

Due to his heavy filming schedule, actor Daniel Radcliffe, was unable to attend the dancing choreography sessions for several of the films. As a result he was unable to keep pace with the other actors.

Shots where Harry is seen dancing focus on his upper body. This was to avoid Harry looking like a clumsy oaf while everybody else appears to dance normally.

If you want to see this for yourself check out the Yule Ball sequence in the Goblet of Fire movie.

My eyes!

In order to make Snape's eyes appear dark and sinister, actor Alan Rickman had to wear contacts. Since he always wore them, and director Mike Newell never Alan putting on his contacts, he just assumed that black was Rickman's natural eye color.

During filming he commented on how great it was that Rickman's eyes were naturally black. Rickman surprised him by popping out his contact and waving it around. For a moment it gave the director quite a fright!

Get off the Treadmill and Back into the Kitchen

Actor Harry Melling was chosen for the role of Dudley Dursley specifically because he was overweight. The directors thought he carried the extra poundage well and didn't look "grossly obese."

But during the months between the Chamber of Secrets and the Prisoner of Azkaban films, Melling went on a diet and started exercising more. He lost so much weight that his portrayal of Dudley would have been completely unrealistic. In the books Dudley does not successfully go on a diet.

Unable to replace the actor, the producers instead built a custom fat suit for him. It was quite expensive. Filmmakers also had to spend hours applying special makeup to his face.

Don't get too Greedy

Remember the character of Rolanda Hooch, aka Madam Hooch? She taught Harry and his friends how to ride a broomstick in the first book.

You might have seen her in the first movie. The character was played by actress Zoë Wanamaker. After the first film she accused the filmmakers of underpaying the actors. Then she demanded more money to appear in the following films.

Unwilling to cough up any more dough, the producers cut her character from the storyline.

Lock my Heart and Throw Away the Key

Heartthrob actor and star of many popular romantic comedies, Hugh Grant, was the first actor cast to play Gilderoy Lockhart.

The contracts were just about to be signed when Grand had to drop out due to scheduling conflicts with *Bridget Jones's Diary*.

He was replaced by Kenneth Branagh, an accomplished stage and film actor, famous for his leading roles in *Henry V* and *Hamlet*.

Professor Whatever

In modern academia, a doctoral degree is usually required to work as a full-time, tenure-track university professor. At Hogwarts you just need a connection with the headmaster.

That's right, there's no set-in-stone qualifications for becoming the professor of Charms or Defense Against the Dark Arts.

J. K. Rowling has said that most of the time you'll need to apprentice under an existing professor, but really it's just at the headmaster's discretion. Like when Dumbledore tracked down Remus Lupin and offered him a job.

Tom the Improviser

Actor Tom Felton improvised many of his own lines. When the movies started filming he wasn't an experienced actor and often forgot his lines. Sometimes he would just shout out whatever came into his head.

For example: In the Chamber of Secrets, Harry drinks a polyjuice potion and transforms himself to look like Malfoy's friend Goyle. Felton forgot his line and said, "I didn't know you could read." This ended up being one of the funnier lines in the movie so the director decided to keep it.

Improvising lines happens a lot in film production. Actors will do short takes and rattle off a bunch of one-liners. In post-production, the editor and the director will sit down and decide which line is best.

That’s a lot of Glasses

More than 300 pairs of prop glasses were used in the creation of the Harry Potter movies. 160 of these were just for Daniel Radcliffe.

At a cost of at least $10 USD, that’s $1,600 just in glasses for Harry. No wonder each movie had a budget of more than $125 million.

Wrong Train

Everyone knows where platform 9 and ¾ leads to. But did you know there is another secret platform at King's Cross Station accessible only to wizards and witches?

Platform 7½ leads to a long-distance sleeping train that stops at various wizard villages around Europe. It's quite similar to the old Orient Express.

Who knows who you'll find riding it.

That's a lot of Wreckage

In the Chamber of Secrets movie, Ron and Harry crash a flying car into the Whomping Willow.

The car is a Ford Anglia. It is a compact car designed and manufactured in the UK. It was produced from 1939 to 1967.

14 custom-modified Ford Anglias were destroyed in the making of the Chamber of Secrets. Each car cost more than £15,000.

Love Potion Symbolism

Many readers often wonder if Voldemort was incapable of feeling love/happiness because he was conceived while his father was under the effects of a love potion.

When asked about this, J.K. Rowling's said: "It was a symbolic way of showing that he came from a loveless union -- but of course, everything would have changed if Merope had survived and raised him herself and loved him."

So there you have it. It's not *impossible* for him to feel love, it's just symbolism, a classic literary device. Symbolism is used to give ideas object or ideas a different meaning that is deeper and more significant than its literal meaning.

Just Like in the Book

Before principal photography began on the Prisoner of Azkaban, director Alfonso Cuarón asked Daniel Radcliffe, Emma Watson, and Rupert Grint to write a short essay on each of their characters.

The director wanted to get inside their head and really understand their motivations. Since the actors had been playing these characters for years, it seemed like a good idea.

Emma turned in a 16 page essay.

Daniel turned a single page with information mostly taken from Wikipedia.

Rupert Grint never turned his in. Now how's that for method acting?

How to Make an Ancient Library

Some of the movie scenes called for magical tomes and huge books, like those found in Dumbledore's library.

To create the prop books, custom covers were created and then aged to look hundreds of years old. Inside the prop book was pages ripped from old phone books.

They reportedly even had trouble finding enough phone books because not really anybody used them anymore.

Real Plants Fake Potions

While you probably know that most of the potions found in the Harry Potter universe are made up, did you know that most of the plants are real? J.K. Rowling used a book on plants and herbs published in 1653 as her inspiration.

The book was *Culpeper's Complete Herbal*. It was written by Nicholas Culpeper, who was a herbalist, physician, and astrologer.

Doesn't he just sound like a character from Harry Potter?

Secondary Career

Over the course of filming the Harry Potter movies, Daniel Radcliffe is reported to have "accidently" broken more than 100 of his custom-designed prop wands.

Apparently he was using them as drumsticks.

He didn't like to destroy other people's wands so he just ended up destroying his. Clearly they weren't sturdy enough if he went through that many of them.

Way too Realistic

Remember the scene in Deathly Hallows where Bellatrix Lestrange tortures Hermione? Well apparently the original footage was so graphic and horrifying that the ratings board told the producers they could leave it in the movie, but that if they did then it would have to be rated R.

An R-rated movie would have drastically reduced sales so the scene was mostly cut. What you see on the DVD is just a tiny portion of what was filmed.

Emma Watson's acting was so good that Helena Bonham Carter (the actress who played Bellatrix) said she was upset and uncomfortable after doing the scene.

Speaking of realism, did you know that most of the homework the children (extras) were doing in the movies was real? The filmmakers tried giving them fake magic-related stuff to scribble on but the kids couldn't act it out convincingly. So they gave them math, and English work.

Happy Birthday Fred and George

Here's a fun fact that most people don't know about Fred and George. They were born on April 1st, which is celebrated in some countries as April Fool's Day, a day when people play pranks and jokes on each other.

Fred and George are the two biggest pranksters in the Harry Potter books. Is it a coincidence they were born on April 1st?

Definitely not.

Not Such an Amazing Wizard After All

If someone asks you what Harry Potter is about, you might reply it's about a boy who goes to school and becomes a great wizard. But did you know that throughout the entire series, especially in the books, Harry Potter does not actually cast that many spells?

In the first book, in charms class, we see him fail at casting *Wingardium Leviosa*. In fact, the only time he successfully casts a spell, if it even counts as a spell at all, is when he tells his broom to go "Up!"

Even when Harry, Hermione, and Ron confront the troll, it's Ron that uses a spell to make the troll drop the club on its head.

Fake Magic Real Food

Most of the time when you see food being used in the movies it's fake. This is because sometimes it takes hours to film a single scene and food spoils quickly.

In the Harry Potter movies however, most of the food you see is real. This was a choice made by the directors to make the Great Hall feast scenes more realistic.

It was quite expensive but made for a better reaction from the child actors. (You have to spit out the fake stuff.)

Creative Control

J.K. Rowling didn't make a lot of crazy demands on the filmmakers when they adapted her work. She understood that film is a different creative medium and while certain details might work fine in the books, they would have to be changed for the movies.

One thing she did insist on was that the entire cast, every single actor down to the last extra, had to be British. The only exception was Verne Troyer, who played the Goblin, Griphook. (They couldn't find a great British actor who was 2 feet 8 inches.)

When the movie was in post-production however, Verne's American accent was dubbed over with a British voice.

Nightmares of Alexandria

Duke Humfrey's Library is the oldest on the planet. You can find it at Oxford University. Because of all the ancient-looking books, this room was used as a set for the “restricted section,” of strange library books.

After being fire-free for hundreds of years, the curators of the library gave the filmmakers special permission to bring fire into the library to film the scene.

They don’t allow any fire or fire-making devices because the books are so old and dry. One spark and the entire library could burn to the ground in minutes.

Thankfully everything went fine.

Werewolf Achievements

Remus Lupin wasn't just the first werewolf to teach at Hogwarts, he was also the first lycanthrope to be awarded the Order of Merlin. This is an extremely prestigious award that has only been given out a few times in history.

Lupin was awarded this honor posthumously after his brave defense of Hogwarts during the Second Wizarding War.

His actions lead to the greater acceptance of werewolves in the wizarding community. "They're not all bad."

The Rowling-King Connection

Despite writing in completely different genres, author Stephen King and J.K. Rowling are good friends. King has mentioned several times that the Harry Potter books are incredibly well-written, entertaining, and awesome.

Both authors have placed Easter eggs in their stories that allude to the other's work.

In 2006, Stephen King and author John Irving launched a mini campaign begging Rowling not to kill off Harry Potter in the final book.

So Much for Prosthetics

While trying to maintain consistency with the books, the filmmakers tried to give Hermione her classic buck teeth. The only problem was actress Emma Watson couldn't speak properly with them in her mouth. All her lines were coming out garbled and unintelligible. The buck teeth idea was abandoned with J.K. Rowling's permission.

Something similar happened with Daniel Radcliffe. In the books Harry Potter has green eyes. Daniel has blue eyes. They tried to give him contact lenses but he kept having an allergic reaction and his face got all puffy and swollen. This idea was also abandoned so movie-version Harry Potter has blue eyes.

Emma Who?

Emma Watson never dreamed of being an actress. She didn't even intend to audition for the role of Hermione. There was an open casting call at her school but she wasn't interested.

Near the end of the day one of her teachers convinced her to try it out and see what happened. Emma Watson was the last girl to audition for the role of Hermione and she knocked it out of the park.

Emma went on to earn millions as an actress and fashion model. She even spoke at the United Nations as a goodwill ambassador for women everywhere.

Americanized Hogwarts

Sure, if you live in the United Kingdom you'll be going to Hogwarts. But what if you live in America? Did you know each region of the world has their own wizarding school?

The American school is called the Ilvermorny School of Witchcraft and Wizardry. It is located in the Berkshires, which is a rural region in the mountains of western Massachusetts.

You can find Ilvermorny surrounded by mist on the highest peak of Mount Greylock.

The characters Porpentina and Queenie Goldstein from the Fantastic Beasts movie were both educated at Ilvermorny.

H and V are What?

That's right, Harry and Voldemort are related to each other. They're both descendants of the Peverell brothers.

But don't worry, they're only something like super-distant cousins.

In fact, most wizards are related to each other if you go back far enough. This is because there aren't exactly millions of them, and most wizards prefer to marry a witch instead of a Muggle.

Early Drafts

In the first draft of Harry Potter, Hermione's last name was Pukcle.

The original title of *Harry Potter and the Goblet of Fire* was Harry Potter and the Triwizard Tournament. J.K. Rowling changed the title after the book was finished and sent off for editing.

The Letter That Must Remain Silent

Everyone knows who Voldemort is. The most powerful Dark wizard. He-Who-Must-Not-Be-Named, etc, etc.

But did you know the letter “t” in his name is silent? That’s right. J.K. Rowling revealed on Twitter that her chief antagonist’s name is pronounced *Voldemor.*

If you listen to the audio book version of Harry Potter you’ll see it’s pronounced the correct way.

R.I.P. L and T

Did you catch the parallel between Lupin and Tonks and James and Lily Potter? If not, don't worry, most people didn't.

Rowling said, "I wanted there to be an echo of what happened to Harry just to show the absolute evil of what Voldemort's doing. I think one of the most devastating things about war is the children left behind. As happened in the first war when Harry's left behind, I wanted us to see another child left behind."

Edward "Teddy" Lupin is like the next Harry Potter. Both his parents die in a wizarding war against Voldemort. There are five letters in this name. The second and third letters are the same.

That's a bingo alright.

So when is *Teddy Lupin and the Magical Plot Device* arriving on bookshelves? Good question.

Diamond in the Rough

J.K. Rowling wasn't always a billionaire. In fact, she was once, "as close to being homeless as you can get." Living off public assistance and trying to raise her children, life was extremely difficult.

After her mother died she sank into a deep depression that lasted months. This depression was her inspiration for the creation of the dementors, the dark wraiths that feed on human suffering and sadness.

Azkaforgetaboutit

Azkaban wasn't always a creepy wizard prison, patrolled by dark wraiths that suck the happiness from you, it actually used to be much worse.

It was originally the home of an evil wizard named Ekrizdis. Like the sirens of Greek mythology, Ekrizdis would lure sailors and ships with flashing lights and other tricks. Muggle ships would crash the island and the men and women would be marooned forever.

The psychotic wizard performed experiments on the sailors. The survivors were tortured to death.

Latin Lessons

Most of the spells in Harry Potter are based on Latin. Some can be translated literally. For example: “Expecto patronum” translates to “I expect protection.”

Accio, the summoning charm, means “I summon.”

Expelliarmus: “Banish weapons.”

Lumos is slightly modified, as the Latin word for lamp is *lumen*.

Nox is Latin for night. *Nox* is the spell used to extinguish your wand after you cast *Lumos*.

Obliviate comes from *obliviscor* which means “I forget.”

Riddikulus is from both the English and Latin word *ridiculous*, which means absurd, laughable, or deserving of mockery.

That’s a lot of Fouls

Did you know there are 700 different fouls in the game of Quidditch? Seekers get fouled more than any other player because catching the Golden Snitch is worth so many points. During the 1473 Quidditch World Cup, all 700 hundred fouls were committed.

The entire list has never been made public for safety’s sake. But here is a short list in case you ever find yourself up against a great Seeker.

Blatching: Flying your broom into an opponent.

Blagging: Grabbing an opponent’s broom to slow him down.

Blocking: Deliberately putting yourself in the way of an opposing Seeker with the intent to cause a crash.

Blurting: Purposely locking your broom handle with another player’s broom.

Bumphing: Smacking a Bludger towards the crowd.

Cobbing: Using your elbows in an unsportsmanlike manner.

Flacking: Sticking your arms or legs into a goal hoop while trying to bat out the Quaffle.

Haversacking: Dunking the Quaffle into a goal hoop instead of throwing it.

Snitchnip: Touching or interacting with the Golden Snitch if you're not a Seeker.

Quaffle-pocking: Interfering with the Quaffle so it doesn't fly normally. This includes puncturing or transforming it.

Stooging: This foul is called if more than one Chaser enters the scoring area.

Some other unnamed fouls: Attacking your opponent with a broom, axe, or club; setting fire to your opponent and/or his broom; releasing blood-sucking vampire bats onto the playing field; attempting to wound or decapitate someone with a broadsword, transforming an opponent into a polecat.

Son of a Potter

In the extended storyline, Harry and Ginny have a son named James Sirius Potter. He is introduced in the stage play, *Harry Potter and the Cursed Child*. (If you can't get tickets you could always buy the screenplay.)

On September 1st, 2015, J.K. Rowling tweeted that James had arrived for his first year at Hogwarts. She also mentioned that the young wizard had been sorted into Gryffindor, just like his father and grandfather.

Swords Can be Fun Sometime Too

Remember Godric Gryffindor? He was one of the four founding members of Hogwarts. Clearly he was an accomplished wizard, but did you know he liked to do his dueling with a sword?

In fact, in an essay on Gryffindor, J.K. Rowling revealed that back in the old days a lot of the dueling was done with swords instead of wands.

Dumbledore and Grindelwald Sitting in a Tree...

One of the most powerful Dark wizards of all time was Gellert Grindelwald. Angry at the statute of secrecy forbidding wizards from using magic around Muggles, he took matters into his own hands.

He tried to start a revolution and committed several horrible acts against the wizarding community, including murder.

Dumbledore defeated him in a legendary duel, but refused to kill him because...Dumbledore was still in love with him. They met when they were young and grew close because of how charming Grindelwald was.

There Can be Only One

Actor Ian McKellen was offered the role of Dumbledore, but he turned it down. It had nothing to do with money or scheduling conflicts. He just didn't want to play another wizard.

He didn't want the young children to be confused if they watched Lord of The Rings and saw him as Gandalf.

Actors don't like to be typecast as it limits the roles they can land in the future.

Secret Codenames

Sometimes to keep a novel's name from leaking to the public, the publisher will give it a codename. To hide the name of the seventh Harry Potter book from nosy reporters, Bloomsbury gave it the codename *Edinburgh Potmakers*.

That was the name used in all interoffice correspondence. So even if a piece of paper accidently flew out a window, nobody would learn the book was named Deathly Hallows.

Codenames are quite common with movies as well. Producers will trademark several names in order to hide the real name, like hiding a needle in a haystack.

For example: When the fourth Indian Jones movie was in production, the following titles were registered as trademarks by Lucasfilm:

Indiana Jones and the City of Gods

Indiana Jones and the Destroyer of Worlds

Indiana Jones and the Fourth Corner of the Earth

Indiana Jones and the Kingdom of the Crystal Skull

Indiana Jones and the Lost City of Gold

Indiana Jones and the Quest for the Covenant

Check Yourself

Director Alfonso Cuarón is Mexican film director, screenwriter, producer, and editor. He directed the Prisoner of Azkaban.

The producers were excited he wanted to work on a Harry Potter movie but there was only one problem. Alfonso was known for having a potty mouth. When things weren't going well on a film set he would curse up a storm.

That was an issue because many of the actors in Harry Potter were children. So the producers put a special clause in his contract forbidding him from swearing. If he had sworn on the set in front of the children he would have had to pay some serious fines.

What a Hypocrite

The Dark Lord isn't just evil, he's also a huge hypocrite. One of the things he hates the most is half-bloods, someone who had a Muggle for one of their parents.

But Voldemort is also a half-blood. His mother was a witch. An unstable and crazy witch who drugged the dark lord's father with a love potion.

So if Voldemort hates half-bloods, does that mean he hates himself?

Angry Birds

Harry Potter and the Half-Blood Prince, the film, was originally scheduled to be released on November 17th, 2008. But midway through August the studio announced the release date for the movie was being pushed back eight months to July 2009.

Fans were so angry at the president of Warner Brothers, Alan Horn, that they sent him hundreds of death threats.

People were upset that the movie was being pushed back purely for monetary purposes. (The studio wanted a summer blockbuster.)

So it wasn't that the filmmakers needed more time to work on the movie, they just wanted more money. Horn tried to blame the delay on the Hollywood writer's strike but most fans didn't buy it.

It was upsetting to a lot of fans since it created a two-year gap between film adaptations. It did however, shorten the time between the Half-Blood prince and Deathly Hallows part 1.

Quidditch Epilogue

Not everyone went to work for the Ministry of Magic after the end of the Harry Potter books.

Ginny Weasley became a professional Quidditch player. She played for the Holyhead Harpies as both a chaser and a seeker.

Eventually she retired to raise her children James, Sirius, and Albus.

She now works as the senior Quidditch correspondent for the Daily Prophet where she's basically she's a sports reporter.

Hogwarts Castle

The castle used for Hogwarts in the movies is Alnwick Castle, in Northumberland, England. This castle has also been used in other movies like, *Robin Hood: Prince of Thieves (1991).*

Unlike in Robin Hood, the castle needed a serious facelift to make it look like an authentic wizarding school. Most of the elaborate stonework you see in the movies is actually plaster and/or computer graphics.

Alnwick Castle is a major tourist attraction and receives more than 800,000 visitors every summer. It is owned by Ralph Percy, 12th Duke of Northumberland. The Duke and his family live in the castle but occupy only a small part of it.

The Riddle Gang

Everyone knows who the Death Eaters are, but did you know they were originally called the Knights of Walpurgis?

The name comes from the date of April 30th, sometimes called Walpurgis Night, a night when witches and demons gather. According to legend anyway.

Voldemort started recruiting his army while he was still in Hogwarts. People like Avery, Antonin Dolohov, and Bellatrix Lestrange.

He used his Hogwarts buddies to help him break into the Chamber of Secrets.

After Tom Riddle became Lord Voldemort, the Knights of Walpurgis became the Death Eaters.

Postscript Ron

After the Second Wizarding War, Ron married Herimone and became an Auror, just like Harry.

After two years he quit his job to go work for his brother, George, at Weasley's Wizard Wheezes which is doing great business.

Rita Skeeter wrote in her column that Ron was tired of living in Harry's shadow, and must be mentally ill to quit his job and go work in a prank store.

Ron's two children are named Rose and Hugo. Rose is currently attending Hogwarts and Hugo yearns to join her.

The Directors Said Forget it

Two famous directors were given the opportunity to direct the first Harry Potter movie, but both passed on it.

The first was Stephen Spielberg, who turned down the opportunity because he was busy with other projects.

The second was M. Night Shyamalan who was recommended by Spielberg, but turned down the job. It was reportedly said because of creative differences. He would not have been able to make many changes to the story/script as he would have liked.

The job eventually went to Chris Columbus, who was famous for directing *Adventures in Babysitting, Home Alone,* and *Mrs. Doubtfire.*

Founding Dark Father

Despite popular belief, the horcrux wasn't invented by Voldemort or Grindelwald. It was created by one of the first Dark wizards. An old man from ancient Greece named Herpo the Foul.

Herpo was also the first wizard to successful breed a Basilisk. (This is not a smart thing to do as very large snakes get hungry and might think you're a snack.)

The Dark wizard avoided getting eaten because he was a Parselmouth, which means he had the ability to talk to snakes.

He was also famous for inventing many vile curses.

Love your Patronus

Several characters change their patronus over the course of the Harry Potter series.

Professor Snape's patronus turned into a doe when Lily Potter died. It changed that way because he was in love with Lily and Lily's patronus was a doe because she was in love with James Potter whose patronus was a stag. Did you get all that? Okay good.

Nymphadora Tonks' patronus was originally a jack rabbit. When she fell in love with Lupin, her patronus changed into a wolf.

Remember, your patronus will always assume the shape of the animal you share the most affinity with.

She-Who-Must-Not-Be-Named

J.K. Rowling has mentioned on several occasions that Dolores Umbridge is "just as evil as Voldemort."

Did you know the cruel inquisitor was based on someone the author knows in real life? Rowling never admitted who it was specifically, but she did say she feels "the purest dislike" for this person.

Thankfully Umbridge ends up in prison for her crimes against Muggles.

The Bride McGonagall

While working at the Ministry of Magic, Minerva McGonagall began to have feelings for her boss, Elphinstone Urquart. He proposed to her several times but she turned him down.

She was still enamored with Dougal McGregor but then he was murdered by Death Eaters during the First Wizarding War.

After that, Minerva accepted a marriage proposal from Elphinstone. They quickly married and were quite happy for three years. Unfortunately he was bitten by a Venomous Tentacula and died.

Many readers suspected she had a thing for Dumbledore until it was revealed he was gay.

She didn't have the best luck with men.

Memorial

J.K. Rowling receives a lot of fan mail, but some is more special than others. She was contacted by a young Canadian girl named Natalie McDonald who was dying of Leukemia. Natalie loved the Harry Potter series and wished to know what would happen to characters because she feared she wouldn't live to the end of the series.

J.K. Rowling wrote back and told Natalie what happens to everyone at the end of Harry Potter. But by the time the letter reached the young Canadian, it was too late. Natalie has passed away.

In her honor, a first-year student was introduced in *Harry Potter and the Goblet of Fire*. The character's name was Natalie McDonald and she was sorted into Gryffindor.

Natalie's mother kept the epilogue information secret for several years until the Harry Potter series was finished.

Lightning Bolts are Neat

On Harry's forehead is a scar in the shape of a lightning bolt. He received the night his parents died.

J.K. Rowling chose the shape because she thought it looked "cool." There was no other reason. It didn't have anything to do with the Killing Curse, or the Horcrux. It was just a neat shape.

Serious Tattoos

When we meet up with Sirius Black in the movies, we see his body is covered in tattoos. These were modeled after Russian prison tattoos.

Other movies have done this as well. In *Eastern Promises*, actor Viggo Mortensen's fake tattoos were so realistic that when he went to a restaurant one night after filming, people left because they thought he was a super-serious high-level gangster.

The Saddest Half-Giant

Despite loving animals, creatures, dragons, and other non-human pets, Rubeus Hagrid cannot conjure a patronus. It's not that he hasn't tried to summon one, or that he doesn't want to, it's a matter of education.

Don't forget, Hagrid was booted from Hogwarts and his wand was snapped in half. He was kicked out of school because he kept an acromantula, a giant sentient spider, as a pet. The spider's name was Aragog. (Tom Riddle framed him for opening the Chamber of Secrets. He also lied about Aragog being the "Monster of Slytherin.")

So it's not that Hagrid wouldn't a want a patronus, it's that he literally can't summon one because he isn't great at casting complicated spells. Hagrid has to make do with living pets like, Buckbeak, Fang, Fluffy, and Norberta.

Hurry it up Already

Sometimes the Sorting Hat takes a while to place a student into a house. If it takes more than five minutes, this is called a "hatstall."

Some notable hatstalls were Minerva McGonagall and Peter Pettigrew.

Harry Potter was *almost* a hatstall, as the Sorting Hat had trouble picking between Gryffindor and Slytherin.

Some People Just Love Harry Potter

Robbie Coltrane, the actor who played Rubeus Hagrid turned down a high-paying recurring role on a TV show so he could keep playing Hagrid.

The role was on Aaron Sorkin's hit series, *The West Wing*. Coltrane would have made a lot more money but he wouldn't have been able to play Hagrid in the second film, or any film after that.

Thankfully, for continuity's sake, he chose Harry Potter.

Another fun fact: Robbie Coltrane as Hagrid was the first role cast in the Harry Potter series.

Mirror Revelations

In the first book, Harry looks into the Mirror of Erised, an ancient ornate mirror with clawed feet. Dumbledore tells Harry the mirror will reveal the "deepest, most desperate desire of our hearts." It shows him a reflection of his parents.

When Harry asks Headmaster what he sees in the mirror, Dumbledore says he sees himself holding a pair of thick woolen socks. Harry suspects he isn't telling the truth.

In an interview, J.K. Rowling reveals that Dumbledore saw his family, happy and reconciled. (His father died in Azkaban. His mother and sister died accidently.)

Vroom Zoom

In the very first chapter of the Sorcerer's Stone, Hagrid appears riding a flying motorcycle. It once belonged to Sirius Black. Two spells were cast on the bike, one to make it larger, and second to make it fly like a broomstick.

During an escape from Death Eaters, the bike is heavily damaged. Not even the *Reparo* spell is able to fix it. The bike ends up in a shed in Mr. Weasley's backyard. Eventually he's able to fix it and gives it to Harry as a gift.

In the movies the bike was a white 1959 Triumph 650 T 120 Bonneville.

Sometimes People get Smashed Together

Some of the characters in the Harry Potter books didn't make it into the movies. Some of the characters were combined to create a new character.

This often happens in book-to-film adaptations because it doesn't make sense to hire three different actors to each say one or two throwaway lines when you can hire one great actor to do it.

For example: The character Nigel Wolpert only appears in the Harry Potter movies. You won't find him in the books. He's the combination of Colin and Dennis Creevey.

Axed from the Show

Some characters from the books never made it to the big screen. Here's a list of characters from the books that were never filmed, or were filmed and had their scenes cut from the final version:

Ludo Bagman, head of the Department of Magical Games and Sports at the Ministry of Magic.

Cuthbert Binns, the History of Magic professor at Hogwarts

Rodolphus Lestrange, Bellatrix Lestrange's husband who was jailed in Azkaban with her. In the movies he doesn't appear at all, and it's implied that Bellatrix has a thing for He-Who-You-Must-Not-Be-Romantically-Involved-With.

Alice and Frank Longbottom, Neville's parents who are tortured and killed by Death Eaters.

Crabbe and Goyle's parents. In the books their fathers are Death Eaters who fight alongside Voldemort.

Marvolo Gaunt, the grandfather of Tom Riddle.

Merope Gaunt, Voldemort's emotional train wreck of a mother.

Peeves, the resident poltergeist of Hogwarts who is always getting into or getting others into trouble.

The Prime Minster of the United Kingdom, one of major point-of-view characters in the books.

Andromeda and Ted Tonks, the parents of Nymphadora Tonks. They helped out the Order of the Phoenix.

Winky, the Crouch family alcoholic house elf.

Army Coins

Dumbledore's Army was created by Harry, Ron, and Hermione. They formed the group because Delores Umbridge refused to teach her students anything about the Defense Against the Dark Arts, beyond textbook theory.

Hermione cast the *Protean Charm* on several coins and gave a coin to each member of the D.A.

This charm linked each coin together. So when they wanted to hold a meeting they would chain the date on the master coin, and it would be reflected on all the coins.

But what you didn't know is...after the Second Wizarding War, all of the students kept their coins. Rowling revealed on Twitter that the coins were like a "badges, or medals of honor," and each student wanted to hold onto them forever.

Happy Birthday to Both of You

Harry Potter's birthday is July 31st. J.K. Rowling's birthday is also July 31st. Coincidence? Probably not.

Here's a fun fact: If there are 23 people in a room, there's a 50% chance that two of them share the same birthday.

It sounds false but it's not. Your brain's just playing tricks on you because it *sounds* impossible.

But look at it this way: If there are 23 people in a room, then that's 253 different pairs to make a comparison between. 253 chances for two people to share the same birthday. Person A has a chance to share a birthday with B, C, D, E, F, etc. And so does Person B. They might share with A, C, D, E, etc. And so on.

As Hermione would say, it's really quite logical when you think about it.

Patronus Games

Ron's patronus is a Jack Russell Terrier. Hermione's patronus is an otter.

The small dogs have been known to chase otters around when they catch them on a dock. Is this a coincidence? Ron annoys Hermione for most of the series and ends up "chasing her" into marriage. Is this a coincidence?

Probably.

J.K. Rowling has said that the otter is her favorite animal. Also that Hermione is probably the character that mimics her real life persona the most.

Dumblegeezer

When Dumbledore dies during the Battle of the Astronomy Tower he's much older than you might think.

Richard Harris, the actor who played Dumbledore in the first and second Harry Potter movies, died when he was 72. In the books, the Headmaster dies at the ripe old age of 150. He wasn't on a special diet, nor did the find the fountain of youth, he was just a wizard, and wizards live longer.

While never officially confirmed, it's possible it has to do with the advancements in healing magic, similar to medical advancements allowing humans to live longer.

Life expectancy for Muggle males is 68 years and 4 months. For females it's 72 years and 8 months.

Japanese Muggles live the longest with an average life expectancy of about 84 years. Maybe it's all the seafood.

The Origin of Quidditch

Sometimes people wonder how author J.K. Rowling came up with the idea for Quidditch. Did she study other sports? Did she spend years perfecting the ultimate game for wizards?

Nope.

She invented Quidditch in a bar on some napkins. If was after she had a humongous fight with her current boyfriend. She stormed out, went to the pub, and the idea just came to her.

Rowling said, “I don't really know what the connection is between the [argument] and Quidditch except that Quidditch is quite a violent game and maybe in my deepest, darkest soul I would quite like to see him hit by a bludger.”

Famous Color Palettes

In the Half-Blood prince film, you'll notice the colors and lighting in each scene are different than the other films.

The art director used Rembrandt paintings for inspiration. Rembrandt was famous for his chiaroscuro style, or paintings with strong light and heavy shadows designed to create depth.

The director thought it would make Hogwarts feel more spooky and serious to reflect the growing power of Voldemort and the Death Eaters.

Too Realistic

Remember that scene in the Order of the Phoenix movie where Harry screams in the Department of Mysteries? That's not actually Daniel Radcliffe's voice.

When the movie was shown to focus groups, the children were disturbed and frightened because the screaming was too realistic and creepy.

The director agreed and Harry's voice was digitally altered.

Not all the Actors Were British

While it's true that all the human actors had to be from the United Kingdom, the animals were another story.

Most of the trained owls were imported from Massachusetts in America.

While the Harry Potter movies were in the theaters, owl adoption went through the roof. Everyone wanted a pet owl. But when the movies were finished, many fans lost interest in keeping the owls as pets and abandoned them at bird sanctuaries.

It seems taking care of an owl is expensive and a lot of work. Not really worth it when it doesn't deliver mail for you.

Marathon

Some people like to throw Lord of Rings viewing parties, and watch each movie back-to-back. The extended editions, of course.

It takes about 11 and-a-half hours to do this. So you need to get started around noon if you want to finish up before midnight.

The Harry Potter series is a whole different beast. If you were to watch all eight Harry Potter movies back-to-back it would take you just about 19 hours.

Some fans have done it. By the end most of them say they were sick to death of Harry Potter.

Dobby the Graphic

Dobby the House Elf is the only character in the Harry Potter movies with a speaking part who is 100% computer animated.

To give the actors something to look at, filmmakers stuck a tennis ball on a stick and waved it about. Dobby was added digitally in post-production.

Harry Potter, The-Boy-Who-Made-Bank

Ever wondered what it would feel like to be a millionaire before the age of 13? Well that's what happened to Daniel Radcliffe. While he may have only been paid $145,000 for the first film, he earned more than $3 million for the second.

Azkaban got him $6 million, and the Goblet of Fire brought in $11 million.

His salary kept jumping with every movie. For each part of Deathly Hallows he got $20 million, so 40 in total.

Not bad for waving a wand around. He is now reportedly worth more than $150 million USD. Emma Watson is worth approximately $60 million, and Rupert Grint is worth about $50 million.

Snowballs

In the first book, Fred and George throw snowballs at Professor Quirrell's turban. What they didn't know was that hiding under the turban was Voldemort.

Voldemort was displeased that Quirrell had failed to steal the Philosopher's Stone from Gringotts. The Dark Lord's disembodied head was hiding under the turban so he could keep a closer watch on Quirrell.

So Fred and George unknowingly hit the most dangerous dark wizard on the planet right in the face with packed snow. Not wise.

You're in the Movie, Trust Me

Jason Isaacs, the actor who played Lucius Malfoy, originally told his agent to pass an offer for *Harry Potter and the Deathly Hallows,* part 1.

When asked why he didn't want to be in the film, he said the reason was that his character was imprisoned at the end of the Half-Blood Prince, and he didn't want to act in a small unimportant role.

After J.K. Rowling assured him his character would be released from prison in the first few scenes, he agreed to sign back on to the project.

Actors are fickle bunch sometimes.

Wait, What? How Does That Work?

Harry Potter and the Order of the Phoenix was by far the longest Harry Potter book. 257,045 words and about 800 pages.

So you'd think it would make the longest movie, but it's actually the shortest movie.

Order of the Phoenix has a running time of only 139 minutes.

The longest film is Chamber of Secrets at 161 minutes. There are only 85,141 words in the book.

Not so Magic Bats

If you're using real owls, why not bats as well? You probably didn't know you could train a bat. But that's just what the filmmakers did.

The bats you see swirling around Hagrid's hut are real live bats. Trainers used pieces of banana on string and fishing line to get the bats to fly around in circles.

Bats will usually fly around in circles if there is something juicy to eat, like bugs. You can see this for yourself if you go to a cottage in the country. Just step outside around dusk and look up.

Woops

Scuba divers use elaborate hand signals to communicate under water. This is a great idea but only if you don't mess up what you're trying to say.

While filming a scene for Goblet of Fire, Daniel Radcliffe accidently flashed a hand signal that said, "I'm drowning."

The emergency rescue team dove into the water and dragged him out. Woops.

Too Long for Cinema

When screenwriter Steve Kloves turned in the first draft of Deathly Hallows, it was over 500 pages long. The general rule is that one page is equal to one minute of screen time. Since most movies run about two hours, most movie scripts are about 120 pages long.

Obviously 500 pages was way too long. But when the producers along with J.K. Rowling tried to edit it down to something manageable, they found it was impossible without cutting major scenes/plot developments. That's why the final movie was broken into two parts.

The final screenplay for each Deathly Hallows movie was about 140 pages long. So about 220 pages ended up being cut from the original 500 page monster.

The Golden What?

Quidditch seekers haven't always chased a Golden Snitch around. Back in the day they used to chase a real bird. It was called the Golden Snidget.

Golden Snidgets are small, bright-yellow plump creatures with rotational wings like a hummingbird. Unfortunately, due to the popularity of Snidget-hunting, the poor bird was on the verge of extinction.

Elfrida Clagg, the Chief of the Wizards' Council, declared the Golden Snidget a protected species. But the problem was players still wanted to chase the Snitch around. It was lots of fun. So metal-charmer Bowman Wright invented the Golden Snitch and that's what we use today.

Makeup can be Tricky

At the end of the Deathly Hallows part 2, there is a 19-years-later epilogue scene. This wraps everything up nicely and we find who got married and all that fun stuff.

The only problem was the makeup. The first time they shot the ending someone in the makeup department messed up big-time. When the film went to post-production the make-up was giving off a terrible shine that actually ruined every single shot.

The entire 19-years-later sequence had to be re-shot. This was very expensive.

It's Hard Being a Teenager

Growing up comes with a lot of complications. Especially *skin* complications.

A lot of the child actors being used as extras and for small parts had terrible acne. Filmmakers tried applying make-up but it didn't look great in the close-up shots.

They tried a bunch of different products, but eventually ended up asking the computer graphics people for help. Anyone with acne with digitally made beautiful in post-production.

Okay Fine I'll Give it a Go

Like Emma Watson, Katie Leung never intended to be an actress. One day she was about to go shopping when her father told her about the open casting call for the role of Cho Chang.

On a whim, she decided to try out for the part. She ended up beating out more than 3,000 other girls. You don't normally get that many people trying out for a secondary character.

Harry Potter is just that popular.

Where the Wild Names Grow

Back in 2000, Scholastic held a question contest and some lucky students got to ask J.K. Rowling a question. One of these questions asked how she came up with all the neat names for people and locations, like the dormitories at Hogwarts.

The author responded, "I invented the names of the Houses on the back of an airplane sick bag! This is true. I love inventing names, but I also collect unusual names, so that I can look through my notebook and choose one that suits a new character."

Protected Assets

It took more than nine years to film all of the Harry Potter movies. During this time the main actors were almost always under a movie contract. Some of stipulations in the contract might seem a little bizarre.

For example: For those nine years the children were forbidden from playing contact sports, even in their spare time. This was because the risk of injury was too high. If an actor was too seriously injured it could jeopardize the entire production. They might have to spend months re-casting someone, and it would look terrible, visually speaking, if the actor who played Ron changed between movies.

So instead the kids learned how to play golf. There was even a driving range right next to the studio, so they got a lot of practice.

Made in the USA
Lexington, KY
08 December 2017